STERLING CHILDREN'S BOOKS
New York

An Imprint of Sterling Publishing
387 Park Avenue South
New York, NY 10016

STERLING CHILDREN'S BOOKS and the distinctive Sterling Children's Books logo are trademarks of Sterling Publishing Co., Inc.

Text and Illustrations © 2014 by Annie Bach
Designed by Andrea Miller

ISBN 978-1-4549-1051-0

Distributed in Canada by Sterling Publishing
c/o Canadian Manda Group, 165 Dufferin Street
Toronto, Ontario, Canada M6K 3H6
Distributed in the United Kingdom by GMC Distribution Services
Castle Place, 166 High Street, Lewes, East Sussex, England BN7 1XU
Distributed in Australia by Capricorn Link (Australia) Pty. Ltd.
P.O. Box 704, Windsor, NSW 2756, Australia

For information about custom editions, special sales, and premium and corporate purchases, please contact Sterling Special Sales at 800-805-5489 or specialsales@sterlingpublishing.com.

Printed in China
Lot #:
2 4 6 8 10 9 7 5 3 1
04/14

www.sterlingpublishing.com/kids

YOU'RE INVITED...

MONSTER PARTY!

by Annie Bach

STERLING CHILDREN'S BOOKS
New York

Monster invited.
Monster delighted.
Monster squeals,

SO EXCITED!

Monster prepare.
Monster brush hair.

Monster picks out underwear.

Monster arrive.
Monster high-five!

Monster joins the disco jive.

Monster spin.
Monster pin.

Monster peeks,
and Monster wins!

Monster **SWOOSH.**
Monster **WOOSH.**

Monster whacks
the candies loose.

Monster munch.
Monster crunch.

Monster eats a buggy lunch.

Monster blow.
Monster whoa!

Monster, watch out! SPLAT!

Oh no!

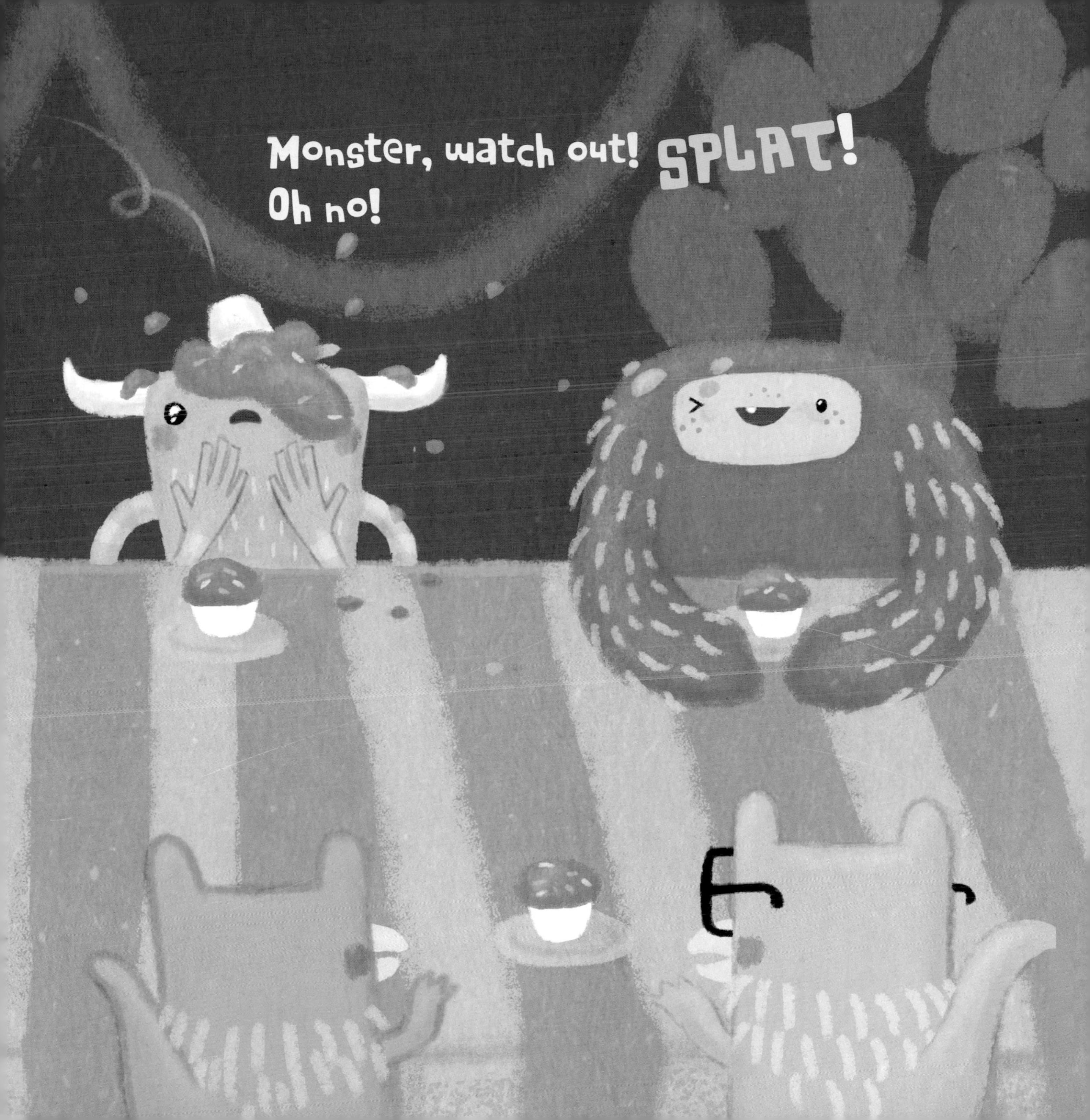

Monsters icky.
Monsters sticky.

Monsters dig in!
(They're not picky.)

Monster unwrap.
Monster clap.

Monster likes his
friend's new cap.

Monster bye. Monster cry.
Monster wipes a teary eye.

Monster pout.

Monster
SHOUT!

Monster huffs
& stomps about.

Monster wail.
Monster tail.

Monster helps
Dad check the mail.

Monster invited.
Monster delighted.
Monster squeals,

SO EXCITED!

YOU'RE INVITED...

Monster glee.
Monster yippee!
Monster marks RSVP.